a Rumpus in the night!

Nick Ward

Albury Children's

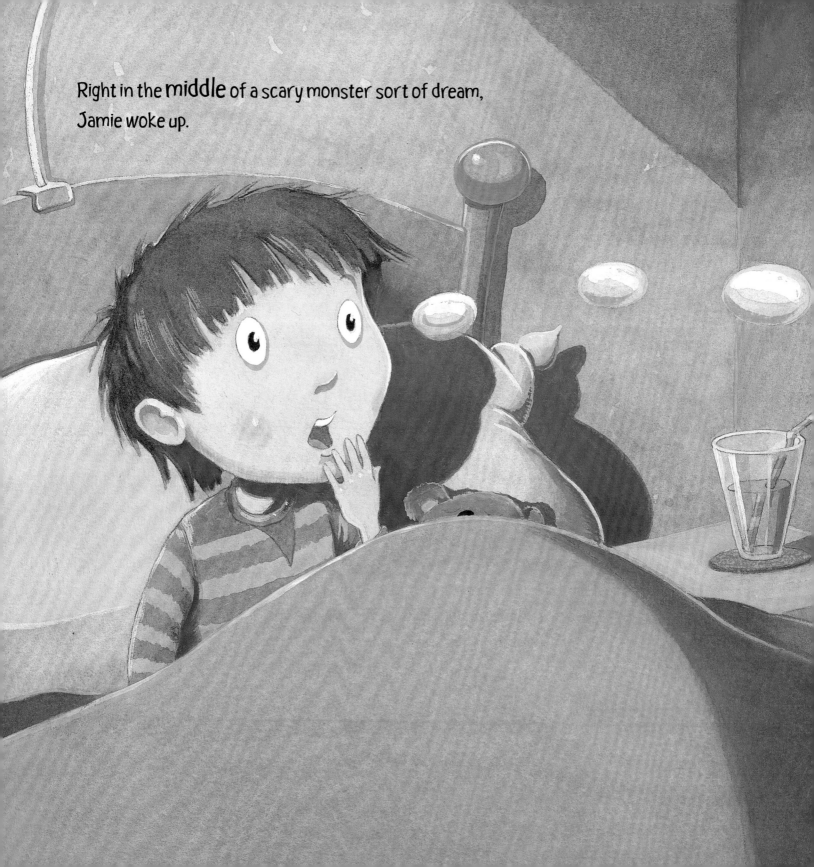

Right in the **middle** of a scary monster sort of dream,
Jamie woke up.

He woke up so suddenly
that part of his dream stayed with him,
and crashing into the bedroom came…

...a **Rumpus!**

It was one of the monsters
from Jamie's dream,
and he looked
VERY surprised!

Jamie was astonished. Surely, hairy little monsters don't get scared, he thought.

"Come out monster, I won't hurt you,"
whispered Jamie, leaning over.

The Rumpus crawled out from under the bed.
"It's dark and I'm frightened and I want to go home," he said.

"You're from my dream," said Jamie.
"How do you get home?"

"You must go back to sleep," snuffled the Rumpus.
"And then I'll pop back into your dream."

"But I'm wide awake now," said Jamie, turning on the light.
"And if I can't get to sleep, Mommy always reads me a story."

"But I can't read," said the Rumpus.

"Then I'll read you a story," said Jamie.
"And then perhaps we'll both fall asleep."

So the Rumpus tried to climb on to Jamie's bed.

"Whoa!" he cried as the covers started to slip.

"Shush Rumpus," whispered Jamie as the monster slid to the floor with a wallop. "You'll wake everyone up!"

"It's not a scary story, is it?" asked a muffled Rumpus from under a tangle of bedclothes. "I don't like scary stories."

Mumf!

Jamie read one story, then another, **then** the first story all over again…
but they were STILL wide awake.

"Sometimes I'm allowed to play a game if I can't sleep," said Jamie.
"Let's play Snakes and Ladders."

BANG!

"**Snakes?**" squealed the Rumpus.

He jumped into the wardrobe to hide and, with a crash, the nervous monster pulled down a rail of clothes.

"I d-don't like s-snakes," came a muffled voice from underneath a pile of coats.

CRASH!

OOF!

"It's only a game," said Jamie.
"Come out and I'll show you."

"I'M THE WINNER!" roared the Rumpus,
marching around the bedroom in triumph.
"Let's have another go… whoops!"
He tripped over the game and sent it flying through the air.

CR

"Shush," said Jamie. "You'll wake everyone up."

"Sorry," whispered the Rumpus. "Aren't you sleepy yet?"

"Not one little bit," sighed Jamie. "Let's play Tag," he said. "You're it!"

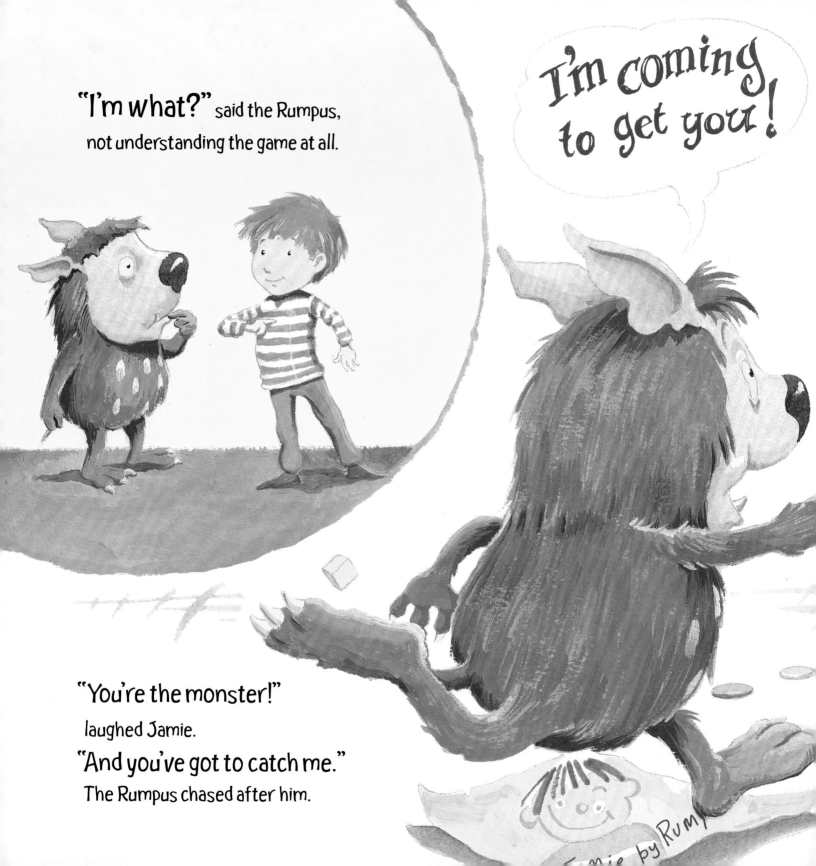

"I'm what?" said the Rumpus,
not understanding the game at all.

"I'm coming to get you!"

"You're the monster!"
laughed Jamie.
"And you've got to catch me."
The Rumpus chased after him.

"You're the monster!" he cried, tagging Jamie.

"NO, you're the monster!"

Then Jamie and Rumpus played
...Follow My Leader! They marched,

...and jumped,

...and skipped.

They bounced on Jamie's bed,
and made a right HULLABALOO...

…until they were completely puffed out.

"I'm not scared anymore," panted the Rumpus, collapsing in a heap.
"Don't go to sleep yet. I want to play some more."

"But I'm so tired," yawned Jamie, crawling into bed. "I'm so…"

"Wake up, Jamie!" cried the Rumpus.

But Jamie fell fast asleep,
and the Rumpus…
disappeared.

MONSTER BOOK

Far, far away in another world,
a **Rumpus** woke up in the **middle**
of a scary monster sort of dream.
He woke up so **suddenly**
that part of his dream stayed with him,
and **crashing** into his bedroom, came...

...Jamie!

For Jimmy!
N.W.

First published in 2004
by Meadowside Children's Books,

This edition published in 2014
by Albury Books,
Albury Court, Albury, Thame, OX9 2LP, United Kingdom

Text ©Beth Shoshan • Illustrations © Piers Harper
The rights of Beth Shoshan and Piers Harper to be identified
as the author and illustrator have been asserted by them in
accordance with the Copyright, Designs and Patents Act, 1988

ISBN 978-1-909958-51-7 (hardback)
ISBN 978-1-909958-30-2 (paperback)

A CIP catalogue record for this book
is available from the British Library
10 9 8 7 6 5 4 3
Printed in China